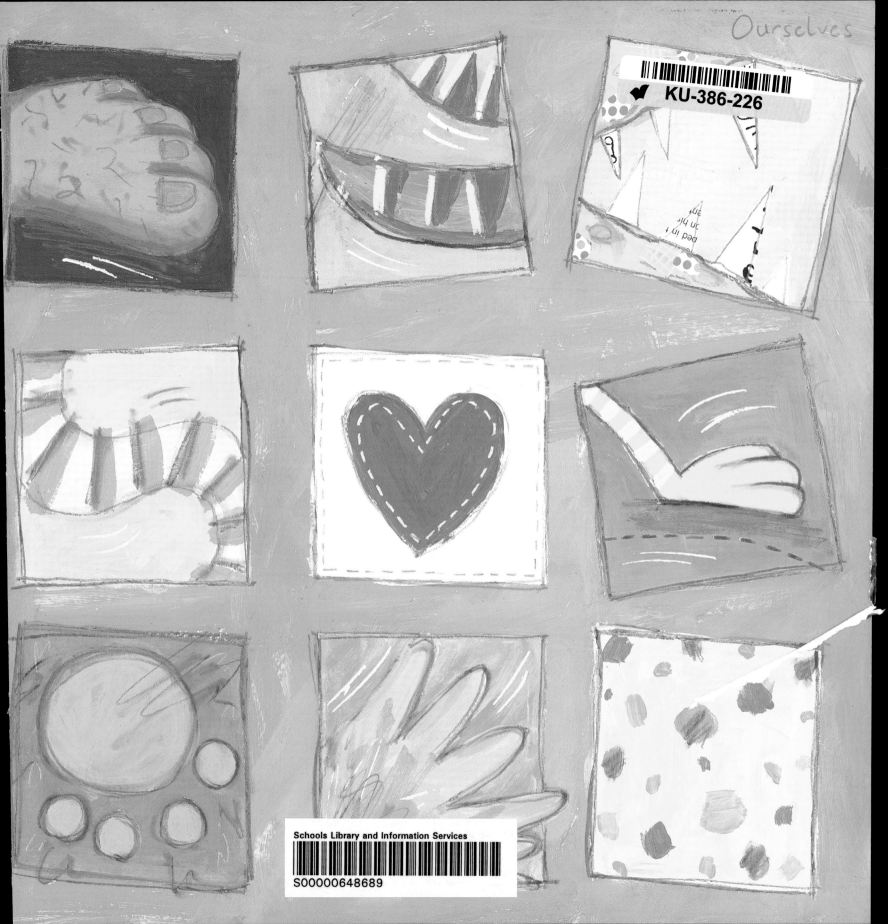

If you're happy

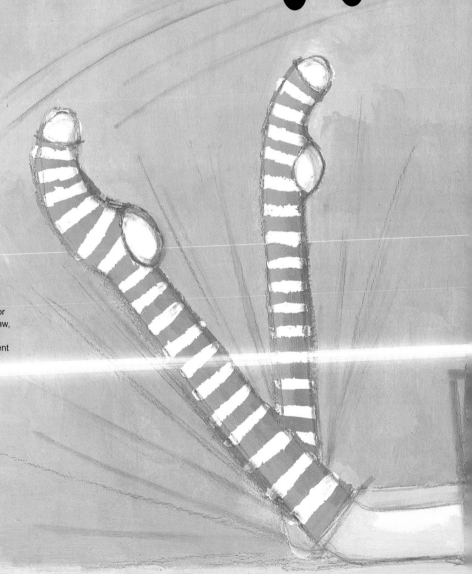

OXFORD
UNIVERSITY PRESS

Great Clarendon Street, Oxford OX2 6DP

Oxford University Press is a department of the University of Oxford.
It furthers the University's objective of excellence in research, scholarship,
and education by publishing worldwide in

Oxford New York

Auckland Bangkok Buenos Aires Cape Town Chennai Dar es Salaam
Delhi Hong Kong Istanbul Karachi Kolkata Kuala Lumpur Madrid
Melbourne Mexico City Mumbai Nairobi São Paulo Shanghai
Taipei Tokyo Toronto

Oxford is a registered trade mark of Oxford University Press
in the UK and in certain other countries

British Library Cataloguing in Publication Data available

ISBN 0 19 279096 X (hardback)
ISBN 0 19 272551 3 (paperback)

1 2 3 4 5 6 7 8 9 10

Typeset in Triplex and Tapioca.

Printed in Singapore by Imago

and you know it!

Jan Ormerod   Lindsey Gardiner

OXFORD
UNIVERSITY PRESS

One day a little girl felt

'If you're happy and you know it, clap your hands.

If you're happy and you know it, clap your hands -

clap, clap!

happy. So she sang,

If you're happy and you know it,

and you really
want to show it...

'No, no, no,' said the small brown dog.

'If you're happy and you know it, wave your tail – swirl, twirl!

If you're happy and you know it, whisk your tail around to show it.

If you're happy and you know it,
wag your tail!'

'My tail is rather insignificant,' said the elephant. **'So I sing,**

If you're happy and you know it,
flap your ears.
If you're happy and you know it,
flap your ears –

flip, flap!

If you're happy and you know it,

'Ridiculous!'
cried the crocodile,
whose ears were very
small indeed.

'If you're happy and you
know it, snap your teeth.

If you're happy and you know it, snap

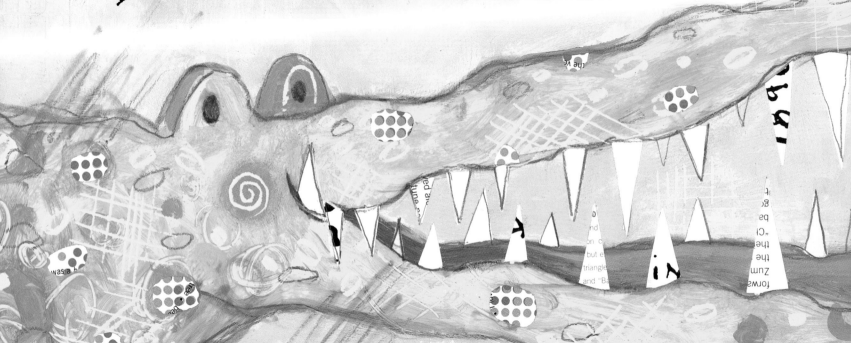

'Or clack your beak?'
called the toucan.

'If you're happy
and you know it,
clack your beak –

'Pathetic,'
said the gorilla.

'If you're happy and you know it,
beat your chest.

If you're happy
and you know it,
pound your chest –
boom, boom!
If you're happy
and you know it,

thump your hairy chest
to show it!'

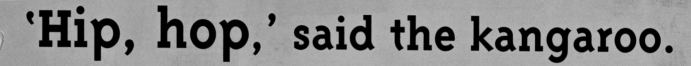

'**Hip, hop,**' said the kangaroo.

'If you're happy and you know it, jump and bump.

If you're happy and you know it, jump and bump –

ping, pong!

If you're happy and you know it,

boing boing along
to show it!'

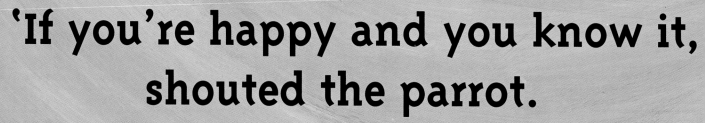

**'If you're happy and you know it,
shouted the parrot.**

'If you're happy and you know it, you should

you should **screech!**'

scream –

hoo!

If you're happy
and you know it,

shriek
and shrill,

scream
and yell.

If you're happy
and you know it,
you should screech.'

The hyena giggled.

'If you're happy and you know it, have a laugh.

If you're happy and you know it, say tee-hee, ha-ha, ho-ho!

If you're tickled and you know it,
chortle, cackle, chuckle, titter.
If you're happy and you know it,
have a tee hee hee.

'So when I'm happy,' laughed the little girl, 'I can do my own thing!'

'That's right,' they all cried.

you know it, do your thing.
you know it, smile and grin.
flap your ears,
snap your teeth,
boom boing.
thing
HOO!

For Lynda, Jen, and Chrissa, BE HAPPY! – L.G.